Montauk Noire
By
Tyler Kenny

Any resemblance to persons living or dead, as well as any location, event, or entity is purely coincidental. This novel is a work of fiction.

Bluebird Publishing—Lindenhurst, NY
ISBN: 979-8-9859987-0-2
Library of Congress Control Number: 2022905898
Title: Montauk Noire and Downtown Op
Author: Tyler Kenny
Available Formats:
Paperback and eBook distribution

This screenplay has been
<u>reformatted</u> for print publication

DO NOT
ENTER
· PROPERTY OF ·
THE STATE OF NEW YORK
AREA CLOSED
TO THE PUBLIC
VIOLATORS WILL BE
PROSECUTED
GER.
UT
IG
TS

EXT. DESERTED STREET   NIGHT

Darkness overwhelms the street. There is a cool,
moist breeze. The faint sound of ocean waves can
be heard. There are a few buildings along the road,
but none have their lights on. Only a few scattered
street lights provide faint light. The area is
deserted until RYAN SCOPIC runs down the street.
He appears scared and desperate.

As Scopic runs, the faint sound of a helicopter
becomes audible. Scopic stops by a street light,
winded. He looks up behind him as the sound of the
helicopter becomes louder. Even more panicked now,
Scopic continues running. As he turns a corner, he
sees a building with a lit doorway. He runs toward
it.

EXT. LIT DOORWAY - NIGHT

Scopic reaches the door. It is made of open glass
and so it is clear that there is nobody inside the
lobby of the building. Scopic bangs on the glass
with his palms.

                         SCOPIC
              Help, I…

Nobody comes to the door. The helicopter is getting
louder. Scopic turns away from the door and starts
to run again when a SHOT rings out, echoing
throughout the vacant street. Scopic is hit in the
head by the gunfire and falls to the ground. As he
lays there, blood pooling, the sound of the
helicopter fades into the distance.

                                        DISSOLVE TO:

EXT. DOORWAY - DAY

The police have gathered around Scopic's body.
There are police cars, crime scene tape, uniformed
officers, and two police detectives named JOHN
MARKS and LEO VERDI. The detectives are examining
the crime scene.

                    MARKS
          So what are we putting in
          the report?

                    VERDI
               (yawns)
          Mugging. Plain and simple.
          Mugger demands his wallet, he
          resists, BAM. Dead. Mugger
          scrams. End of story.

                    CONNOR
               (O.S.)
          That's a great story.

The detectives turn to see CONNOR, a well dressed
and confident looking man strolling toward them.

                    CONNOR
          Don't you think you're a
          little old for fairytales
          though Verdi?

                    VERDI
               (contemptuously)
          Connor. What the hell are you
          doin' here?

Connor reaches the men. As he speaks to them he is
observing the crime scene.

                    CONNOR
          My job. And yours too by the
          looks of it.

                    VERDI
          Yeah well we don't need you. Why
          you interested in some two-bit
          homicide anyway?

                    CONNOR
                (sarcastically)
          A man was killed Verdi. Have
          you no concern for the general
          public?

                    VERDI
          I'll tell ya what I'm
          concerned about you sonofa-

                    MARKS
          Alright settle down Leo.
                (turns to Connor)
          Stiff's name is Ryan Scopic. He
          was killed last night around 1 AM.
          No witnesses. So, what do you make
          of it Connor?

Connor steps past the men toward the body of
Scopic. He crouches down and removes his
sunglasses. He first looks over the body, then
looks up to see a hole in the glass door behind it.
The hole is about two feet above the bottom of the
door. Connor then stands up and turns to face the
detectives.

                    CONNOR
                (as he turns)
          So...what do we know about the
          helicopter?

                    MARKS
          Helicopter?

                    VERDI
          What helicopter?

                    CONNOR
          The one the victim was shot
          from.

                    VERDI
          What the hell makes you think he was
          shot from a damn helicopter?

                    CONNOR
          The hole in the door over there

is clearly from the gunshot. At
the angle the victim was shot
from the killer would have to be
very high up. Since there
aren't any very high buildings
around here, the killer would
have to either be in a
helicopter or be about 12 feet
tall.

                    VERDI
          How is he supposed to
          mug the guy from a
          helicopter?

Connor blinks in an exaggerated and exasperated
manner.

                    CONNOR
          I'm assuming the motive
          wasn't theft.

                    MARKS
          What do you think it is?

                    CONNOR
          Don't know yet. But the last
          homicide incident in this
          town was a year ago when some
          guy was arrested for a murder
          he committed 18 years
          earlier in South Carolina.
          And that's been the only
          homicide incident in this
          town for over 40 years.

Connor smiles.

                    CONNOR
          This should be interesting.

                    VERDI
          Ah, you're nuts. I'm writin'
          this up as a mugging. 'Cause
          that's what it is.

                    CONNOR
          Well at least it should be
          easy to find a 12 foot tall
          perp. Good luck pal.

Connor slides his sunglasses back on and walks
away.

EXT. STREET - DAY
Connor walks down the street, away from the
building.
                    MARKS
          Connor!

Marks trots to catch up to Connor. Connor stops to
see what he wants.

                    MARKS
          Listen Connor...I want
          you to lay off this
          case.

                    CONNOR
          What are you convinced in that
          genius' mugging theory? Come
          on Marks this is the kind of
          case you need me on.

                    MARKS
          Don't worry about him. I'm lead
          detective on this case and I'll
          be sure it gets done right. Now
          the department isn't hiring you
          to look into this so just drop
          it, alright?

                    CONNOR
          Yeah...sure.

Connor walks away. Marks turns and heads back to
the crime scene.

EXT. CONNOR'S CAR   DAY

Connor drives down a road that is close to the
beach. It's a sunny summer day. He then drives into
town and stops by a pancake house.

INT. PANCAKE HOUSE - DAY

Connor sits alone at a booth. He is reading a
newspaper article about Scopic's murder. A young
WAITRESS comes to his table.

                    WAITRESS
          Hi. Start you out with some
          coffee?

Connor puts down his paper and looks up at the
waitress.

                    CONNOR
          No, I'll have a Coke.

The Waitress looks skeptical.

                    WAITRESS
          Isn't it a little early for soda?

                    CONNOR
          Let me worry about that
          sweetheart. And get me some eggs
          with that. Scrambled.

The Waitress smiles at him.

                    WAITRESS
          Coming up.

EXT. CONNOR'S OFFICE - DAY

Connor drives up to his office and parks. It is a
small and modest building. A sign outside reads
CONNOR PI. Connor gets out of his car and enters
the office.

INT. CONNOR'S OFFICE - DAY

Connor walks into the reception area. His
receptionist, AMY, looks up as he enters.

                    AMY
          There you are. I've been
          trying to get you on your cell.

                    CONNOR
          I had it off. I hate the damn
          thing. What's up, Amy?

                    AMY
          There's a Mrs. Scopic here to
          see you.

Upon hearing the name, Connor is mildly surprised,
as he remembers the victim's name from earlier that
day.

                    AMY
          She's been waiting for almost
          twenty minutes. She's in your
          office.

                    CONNOR
          Alright Thanks doll.

Connor heads toward his office.

INT. CONNOR'S INNER OFFICE - DAY

As Connor enters his inner office, BETTY SCOPIC,
a beautiful young woman wearing dark clothing and
a veil, stands from the chair in front of Connor's
desk. She holds a handkerchief and her mascara is
running slightly.

                    CONNOR
          Hello Mrs. Scopic.

                    BETTY
          Mr. Connor.

Connor walks to Betty and offers his hand. She
shakes it.

                    CONNOR
               (doing his best to sound
                sincere)
          I heard about your husband. I'm
          terribly sorry.

                    BETTY
          Thank you.

Connor walks around his desk and sits behind it
as he speaks. He gestures for Betty to sit as well
and she does.

                    CONNOR
          I'm sorry to keep you waiting
          for so long. I know this must be
          a difficult time for you.

                    BETTY
          Yes, well, it was very
          important that I see you.

                    CONNOR
          Oh?

                    BETTY
          You see I wish to hire you to find
          out who killed my husband.

Connor looks mildly surprised.

                    CONNOR
          You don't trust the police to
          handle the case?

                    BETTY
          Actually, it was my
          husband. You see you're
          in his will.

Betty reaches into her handbag and pulls out a
folder. She hands Connor the folder. He opens it
and takes a look.

                    BETTY
          In the event that he
          was...well he wanted a
          private agency handling his
          case. He didn't trust the
          police to find his...his...

Betty starts to weep. Connor becomes visibly
uncomfortable with this. After a moment, he
reaches across the desk to put a hand on her
shoulder.

                    CONNOR
          All right. It's all right. Look
          I'll take the case don't you
          worry.

After a moment Betty stops crying.

                    BETTY
          Oh. Thank you. I'm sorry I've
          just been a wreck since they
          called me.

                    CONNOR
          Not at all. I understand. Mrs.
          Scopic, I need to ask you a few
          things that may help me with your
          case.

Betty hesitates a moment.

                    BETTY
          Alright.

Connor takes out a notepad and paper.

                    CONNOR
          What type of work did your
          husband do?

                    BETTY
          He was a writer. He would write
          articles for newspapers and
          websites.

Connor writes this down.

                    CONNOR
          Did he have any enemies?

                    BETTY
          No, not that I know of. Of
          course he didn't talk to me much
          about his work.

                    CONNOR
          What was the last thing you
          remember him working on?

Betty thinks for a moment, trying to remember.

                    BETTY
          He wrote an article a few weeks ago
          ... something about gas prices.
          How the rise in prices was largely
          the result of taxes.

                    CONNOR
          Did you know that your husband
          expected that this might happen?

                    BETTY
          Oh no of course not. I only found
          out about the will a few hours
          ago.

Connor writes down this last bit and looks up.

                    CONNOR
          Well, that should do it for now.

Betty stands and Connor follows suit. They move to
the door.

                    BETTY
          Well I must be going. I
          need to make
          arrangements for my
          husband.

                    CONNOR
          Of course.

                    BETTY
          Please call me when you
          get any information.

                    CONNOR
          I will. Just leave your
          number with my secretary
          on your way out.

                    BETTY
          Oh thank you Mr. Connor.
          You're very kind.

                    CONNOR
          Not at all Mrs. Scopic.

Betty leaves the inner office and Connor walks back
to his desk and sits down. He stares at the ceiling,
contemplating.

INT. MEDICAL CARE CENTER - DAY

Marks and Verdi are standing on one side of an
examination table and a DOCTOR stands on the other
side. Connor enters the room.

                    CONNOR
          Hey fellas.

                    VERDI
          Great. You again. Would you get
          lost.

                    MARKS
          Leo shut up. Connor I told you,
          the department's not hiring you
          for this.

Connor walks over to the table.

                    CONNOR
          Yeah well, I've been hired by
          Scopic's widow. Her husband
          somehow got the idea that you boys
          aren't very good at your jobs.

Marks has been patient but begins to look
frustrated.

                    MARKS
          Look, I'm ordering you off this
          case.

                    CONNOR
          Well it's a good thing I'm a PI and
          can choose to be on whatever case
          I want. So your orders mean squat.

                    MARKS
          Dammit!

The room is quiet for a moment. Although Connor
seems unperturbed, the doctor looks
uncomfortable, and even Verdi is a little stunned
by Marks.

                    MARKS
          Fine. Do what you want. Verdi,
          let's get out of here.

Marks and Verdi walk to the exit. Marks focuses on
the door as he storms out and Verdi glares at
Connor. After they leave, Connor turns toward the
doctor.

                    CONNOR
          So, what've we got.

The doctor, still shaken from the heated
discussion, takes a moment to answer.

                    DOCTOR
          Well, it's a high caliber
          bullet wound to the head. No
          other signs of injury.

Connor frowns.

                    CONNOR
          Not much to go on.

The doctor shrugs.

                    DOCTOR
               Sorry.

INT. CONNOR'S INNER OFFICE - NIGHT

Connor is working on a laptop. He is reading the
article Betty mentioned about gas prices. There
is a photo attached to the article of a gas station
in town. Under the photo it reads PHOTOGRAPHY BY
SUSIE ROGERS. Connor is visibly interested by
this. He hits the intercom button.

                    CONNOR

          Amy?

Amy answers through the intercom.

                    AMY (O.S.)
          Yes?

                    CONNOR
          Amy get me Susie Rogers' address,
          PDQ. I want to get out
          there before dark.

                    AMY (O.S.)
          Right away.

Connor gets up, puts his jacket on, and picks up
his sunglasses. Amy enters after a moment holding
a paper with the address. She walks to Connor and

holds it out to him.

                    AMY
          Here it is.

Connor grabs the paper.

                    CONNOR
          Thanks sweetheart.

                    AMY
          So what are you goin' out there
          for at this hour? You know, I'm
          not doin' anything tonight.

                    CONNOR
          Well, this is business not
          pleasure. So I'll have to take a
          rain check kiddo.

Connor kisses her on the forehead and heads out of
the office. Amy stands there for a moment, beaming.

EXT. CONNOR'S CAR - DAY

The sun is starting to set as Connor drives toward
Susie's house.

EXT. SUSIE'S HOUSE - DAY

Connor pulls up to her house and gets out of his
car. When he reaches her door, he rings her bell.
After a moment the door opens and Susie stands in
the doorway.

                    SUSIE
               (a little surprised)
          Connor.

                    CONNOR
          Hey darlin'. How are ya?

                    SUSIE
          Alright. Whatcha doin' here?

                    CONNOR
          I'm workin' a case.
          You're name came up.

                    SUSIE
               (a little disappointed)
          Oh.

She hesitates a moment.

                    SUSIE
          Come in.

Connor enters her house.

INT. SUSIE'S HOUSE - NIGHT

The house is small and quiet. A few professional
looking photographs are blown up to poster size and
adorn the walls in frames.

                    SUSIE
          Is this about what happened to
          Ryan?

                    CONNOR
          Yeah. I ran across an article he
          wrote that had one of your
          pictures. Did you work with him
          often?

Susie sits on the couch and gesture for Connor to
sit next to her, which he does. He then takes out
his notepad and begins to take notes.

                    SUSIE
          Oh sure. His articles are very
          inspiring.
               (pausing a moment)
          Were very inspiring I guess. It's
          terrible what happened to him.

                    CONNOR
          Yeah. Well I was hired to find out
          how that happened. You got any
          ideas for me?

                    SUSIE
               (incredulously)
          Oh, no. I can't image anyone
          wanting to hurt Ryan. This
          whole thing is just so
          shocking.

Connor looks up from his notepad and eyes her with
a somewhat skeptical look.

                    CONNOR
          Right. So do you know what he was
          working on before he was killed?

Susie stands up, turns away, and walks across the
room.

                    SUSIE
          No, I haven't worked with him for
          a couple of weeks now.

Again skeptical, Connor responds cautiously

                    CONNOR
          Did you know him...socially?

Susie turns to face Connor.

                    SUSIE
               (defensively)
          What do you mean?

                    CONNOR
          I mean how... intimate was your
          relationship?

Susie furrows her brow and frowns.

                    SUSIE
          Not at all. We never... We were
          colleagues and nothing more. Why
          would we... I mean have you seen
          his wife?

                    CONNOR
               (grinning)
          I sure have. She's the one who
          hired me.

Susie's frown doesn't break.

                    SUSIE
          You can be a real asshole
          sometimes Ty, you know that?

                    CONNOR
               (without hesitation and
               more manner-of-fact than
               guilty)
          Yes.

Susie rolls her eyes dramatically and
turns away again. Connor stands up.

                    CONNOR
          Look I need your help
          here. Whoever killed Scopic is
          powerful and ruthless and I
          need you to give it to me
          straight. What was he working
          on?

Susie is silent for a moment.

                    SUSIE
               (hesitantly)
          There's a military base in the
          park. It's supposed to be
          abandoned but Ryan said he found
          some evidence that it wasn't.

Connor walks over to Susie.

                    CONNOR
          Where would he keep that
          evidence?

                    SUSIE
          I don't know.

                    CONNOR
               (sincerely)
          Alright.

Connor turns and starts walking to the front door.

                    CONNOR
          Thanks for the info
          sweetheart. Call me if you think
          of anything else.

                    SUSIE
          Wait.

Susie follows Connor to the door.

                    SUSIE
Do you have to leave right now?

Connor smiles. He leans in and kisses Susie.

INT. CONNOR'S OFFICE - NIGHT

Amy is putting on her jacket and grabbing her
handbag when Connor walks in.

                    AMY
          There you are. I was wondering
          what happened to you.

                    CONNOR
          Yeah. Before you go can you grab
          me Mrs. Scopic's number?

                    AMY
          Sure.

Connor walks to his inner office.

INT. CONNOR'S INNER OFFICE - NIGHT

Connor sits at his desk. Amy comes in with the
number.

                    CONNOR
          Thanks doll. Have a good night.

                    AMY
          Kay. You too.

Amy leaves. Connor takes out his phone, turns it
on, and calls the number.

                    BETTY (O.S.)
          Hello?

                    CONNOR
          Mrs. Scopic? It's Mr. Connor.

                    BETTY (O.S.)
          Oh, hello. Do you have any news?

                    CONNOR
          Yeah it turns out your husband
          might have gathered some evidence
          to implicate his killer. He would
          probably want to keep it hidden.
          Do you know where it might be?

                    BETTY (O.S.)
          I don't know... He may
          have kept it in his
          safe.

                    CONNOR
          Why don't you check for me?

                    BETTY (O.S.)
          Okay.

There is a pause.

                    BETTY (O.S.)
          I found something about
          a military base.

Connor leans forward in his chair.

                    CONNOR
          That's it! When can you
          get it to me?

                    BETTY (O.S.)
          Tomorrow morning?

                    CONNOR
          Great. Meet in my office
          tomorrow morning.
          Goodnight Mrs. Scopic.

                    BETTY (O.S.)
          Uh, ok. Goodnight.

Connor closes his phone. He leans back in his chair
and closes his eyes.

INT. CONNOR'S INNER OFFICE - DAY

Connor is asleep on his desk. There is a soft knock
at the door. He wakes up, slowly at first then,
realizing someone is at the door, and stands up
quickly. He walks out of his inner office rubbing
his eyes.

INT. CONNOR'S OFFICE - DAY

He walks to the main office door and opens it. He
ushers Betty inside. She is carrying a bag.

                    CONNOR
          Come in. Come in. Sorry
          for the wait, my
          secretary isn't in for
          another half hour.

                    BETTY
          Oh, I'm sorry did I come too early?

They walk to Connor's inner office.

                    CONNOR
          Not at all. I'm anxious
          to see what you've
          brought.

Betty pulls a folder out of her bag.

                    BETTY
          Well, here it is.

Connor takes the folder, opens it, and looks
through it excitedly. Betty speaks as he scans
through the folder's contents.

                    BETTY
          Do you think this will help you
          find my husband's killer?

Connor reads through the folder. He closes it and
looks up.

                    CONNOR
          I got to get over to the
          park. This is the break we've been
          waiting for.

He gets up, puts on his jacket, and walks around
his desk toward the door. As he passes around his
desk, Betty stands up as well.

                    BETTY
          Wait. Isn't that dangerous? I
          mean you have this evidence you
          can use that can't you?

                    CONNOR
          Mrs. Scopic-

                    BETTY
          I mean I don't want the same thing
          to happen to someone else. To you.

Betty touches Connor's chest. Connor takes her
hand and holds it.

                    CONNOR
          Don't worry I can take care of
          myself. I'll be fine Mrs. Scopic.

                    BETTY
          Betty.

                    CONNOR
          Betty. I'll be back here soon.

Connor lets go of her hand and leaves the office.

EXT. CONNOR'S CAR - DAY

Connor drives through the park. It is mostly deserted
and there are many small buildings labeled "DO NOT
ENTER." Eventually, a large building with a large
satellite dish on top comes into view. Connor drives
into a parking lot that overlooks it and parks the
car.

EXT. PARK - DAY

Connor gets out of the car. He looks at the building
in the distance. Suddenly, a shot rings out. The
ground next to Connor bursts from a gunshot. Connor
quickly runs behind his car, keeping low. He pulls
out a snub nosed revolver.

After a moment, he leaps to his car door, opens it,
and enters his car. As no more shots ring out, he
makes his way closer to the building.

EXT. BUILDING - DAY

Connor pulls up to a barbed wire fence, parks his
car, and gets out. From his trunk he pulls a large
mat. He throws it on top of the fence and uses it
to scale the fence.

He runs up to a door and pulls out his gun. He tries
to open the door. It is locked so he kicks it open.
As soon as he does, someone starts shooting at him
from inside. Connor quickly hides out of the line of
fire. The gunfire stops and Connor hears footsteps
running away. He enters the building.

INT. BUILDING - DAY

Connor enters a small lobby in the building. He
runs to the corner of the lobby, which leads to a
hallway. He holds his gun out around the corner and
nothing happens. He looks around the corner and no
one is there.

He turns the corner and runs down the hallway. He
comes to the end and reaches some open double
doors. As he runs in front of them, he is fired upon
again. He slips and falls on his back to avoid the
gunfire and pulls himself around the corner to
hide. He hears footstep running upstairs.

Connor turns the corner and runs up the stairs. He
notices a gun discarded on the staircase and keeps
running. On the next floor he tackles the shooter
to the ground. It is Marks.

                    MARKS
          Damn it. I told you to
          stay out of this Connor.

Connor gets up and points his gun at Marks.

                    MARKS
          Ok, think here Connor.
          I'm a cop. What are you
          going to do? Shoot me?
          Arrest me? Use that big
          brain of yours.

Connor, keeping his gun trained on Marks, turns him
on his stomach and starts patting him down.

                    CONNOR
          You shot at me there, buddy.

                    MARKS
          It was a warning shot! I
          was trying to scare you
          off!

                    CONNOR
          And the ones in the hallway?

Marks is silent. Connor takes out Marks' wallet and
inspects it. Inside he finds a check from Betty
Scopic.

                    CONNOR
          This is quite a lot of money
          Scopic's widow paid you. Now what
          could that be for?

                    MARKS
          You've got nothin' on me or her.

                    CONNOR
          I got this check and that's
          plenty.

                    MARKS
          The lady collected a bundle from
          a life insurance policy on her
          husband. There's no way you're
          gonna be able to hold me or her
          for long. We'll get bailed out
          and disappear.

Connor picks Marks up off of the ground, gun still
trained on him.

                    CONNOR
          Yeah, you're probably right. But
          I'm still gonna do my job. Now
          walk.

EXT. BEACH - NIGHT

The beach is dark and deserted except for Connor,
who stands watching the ocean. Betty walks over to
him.

                    BETTY
          Your secretary said you wanted to
          meet me here Mr. Connor. Did you
          find out who killed my husband?

                    CONNOR
          Yeah we got him. You know I really
          like the beach at night. There's
          just something peaceful about
          it.

                    BETTY
          Who killed my husband Mr. Connor?

                    CONNOR
          A cop named Marks. He
          used a police chopper
          and rifle. You see he
          was hired to do it. By
          you.

                    BETTY

          What? No! I would never-

                    CONNOR
          I know all about it.
          Marks confessed. You
          wanted to make it
          look like the
          government killed off
          a conspiracy wacko to
          throw the scent off
          yourself.

Connor gives Betty a disappointed look.

                    CONNOR
          Why'd you do it Betty?

Betty hesitates, then starts to break down in
tears.

                    BETTY
          He was crazy! Obsessed! He was
          bleeding money. We were going to
          lose everything. I had to do it!

                    CONNOR
          Then why did you hire me?

                    BETTY
          You really were in his will. It
          would look suspicious if I
          didn't...

                    CONNOR
          Damned if you do, damned if you
          don't.

Betty falls into Connor's arms. She looks up at him
through tears.

                    BETTY
          Please don't turn me in. Please.
          I regret what I did. I feel
          terrible all the time. Please.

Betty kisses Connor. Connor pulls her away from
him. He reveals a tape recorder in his jacket
pocket.

                    CONNOR
          Sorry, Betty. It's my job.

Connor leads Betty away by the arm.

                                        CUT TO BLACK

DOWNTOWN OP

Downtown Op

By

Tyler Kenny

EXT. BATTERY PARK   DAY

It's a cold morning in Battery Park. Ferries are
taking tourists to see Ellis and Liberty Islands.
The Statue of Liberty herself stands in the
distance. CONTROL, a handsome man in his 50s sits
on a bench looking out at her. JOHN, a younger man
in his 20s walks over and sits next to him. Neither
man looks at the other.

                    JOHN
          Well?

                    CONTROL
          We're taking you off the ITOS.
          Putting you on CE.

                    JOHN
               (puzzled)
          Why?

                    CONTROL
          Russia House has a leak.
          We need someone new.

                    JOHN
               (sighing)
          I thought the Cold War was over.

                    CONTROL
          The first one is. Every hear of
          the Illegals Program?

                    JOHN
          OK. So?

                    CONTROL
          Here.

Control hands John a folder. He opens it and pulls
out a photograph of KATYA, a beautiful young woman
in her 20s. John looks at the photo with mixed
feelings.

                    CONTROL
          That's Ekaterina Petrova.
          We have reason to believe
          she is working for Russian
          Intelligence and that she
          is getting information from
          our mole.

                    JOHN
          And you want me to find your mole.

                    CONTROL
          Yes. Get close to her. See
          if she can lead you to her
          handlers. (grinning)
          Your kind of assignment, no?

                    JOHN
          No. Can't you give
          this to someone else?

                    CONTROL
               (surprised)
          It's a done deal.
          Honestly, I thought you'd
          jump at the chance to…

Control thinks for a moment then grins again.

                    CONTROL
          Ah. So what's her name?

John, annoyed, gets up to leave. He replaces the
contents of the folder.

                    CONTROL
          What? You don't trust me?

John looks at Control.

                    JOHN
          Is there a reason I should?

Control chuckles to himself as John walks away.

EXT. JOHN'S APARTMENT - DAY

John walks up to the apartment and enters the
building.

INT. JOHN'S APARTMENT - DAY

John enters his apartment closing the door behind
him. He takes the folder from his jacket and places
it in a draw. He enters the kitchen where RENEE,
a pretty woman in her 20s, sits at the table in her
bathrobe, drinking coffee.

                    RENEE
          Morning.

                    JOHN
          Morning.

John moves to the refrigerator to get a water
bottle.
                    RENEE
          Where were you?

                    JOHN
          Couldn't sleep. Went for a walk.

                    RENEE
               (tired)
          You don't want breakfast, do
           you?
                    JOHN
          No. I'm going back to bed.

                    RENEE
          Whatever. I have to get
          ready for work.

John heads to the bedroom.

EXT. CENTRAL PARK - DAY

Katya is sitting by a baseball field reading a
paper. John walks over and sits down next to her.
She looks up from her paper to him. He smiles at
her and she smiles back.

                    JOHN
          Hi.

                    KATYA
          Hello.

John nods his head toward the ball field.

                    JOHN
          Do you play?

                    KATYA
               (laughing)
          Sometimes for fun. I love your
          baseball. How about you?

                    JOHN
          Yeah my dad taught me to play. I'd
          play with him or my friends on
          weekends. Just pickup games, you
          know, but it was fun. I'm John by
          the way.

John reaches out his hand and Katya shakes it.

                    KATYA
          Katya. Nice to meet you.

EXT. OUTDOOR CAFE - DAY
Katya and John sit at a table. They are drinking
coffee, smiling, chatting, and laughing.

INT. JOHN'S APARTMENT - DAY

Renee and John sit at the kitchen table. They are
quiet, sipping from mugs of coffee, and reading the
paper.

EXT. RESTAURANT - NIGHT

Katya and John sit in a quiet, romantically lit
restaurant. He holds her hand in his. Their eyes
meet and they smile.

INT. JOHN'S APARTMENT - NIGHT

Renee pulls a TV dinner out of the microwave and
puts it on the kitchen table in front of John.

EXT. PHONE STORE - DAY

Katya comes out of a cellphone store with a box for
a new phone. She takes her receipt and throws it
into a nearby trash can. As she walks away, John
comes from around the corner and grabs the receipt
out of the trash can.

EXT. SOUTH SHORE SEAPORT - DAY

John and Control are sitting on a bench. John
covertly passes Control the receipt. Control takes
it and puts it in his jacket pocket.

INT. NIGHTCLUB - NIGHT

Katya introduces John to some of her friends, three
men and one woman. John shakes their hands.

People are dancing on the dance floor.

John is talking with one of Katya's male friends.
He pours the man another drink and motions for him
to continue.

INT. NIGHTCLUB BATHROOM   NIGHT

John is in a stall writing down names and other
information on a notepad.

INT. NIGHTCLUB - NIGHT

John comes out of the bathroom and goes back to the
group. Just as he sits down, Katya comes over and
playfully pulls him by the arm. He stands and she
leads him to the dance floor where they begin
dancing.

EXT. SOUTH SHORE SEAPORT - DAY

John hands Control the list he wrote in the
bathroom.

INT. JOHN'S APARTMENT - NIGHT

Renee and John sit apart from each other on the
couch watching television. Renee seems mildly
interested in the program, but John is very bored.

INT. NIGHTCLUB - NIGHT

John is dancing very closely with Katya. They look
into each other's eyes and kiss each other.

INT. JOHN'S APARTMENT - DAY

John is putting his coat on. Renee sits at the
kitchen table in her bathrobe.

                    RENEE
          You wanna rent a movie tonight?

                    JOHN
          I dunno. I might be home late.
          Don't wait up, alright?

John leaves the apartment. Renee sits alone at the
kitchen table.

INT. KATYA'S APARTMENT - DAY

Katya is cooking something on the stove in the
kitchen. John walks up behind her and holds her
waist, looking down at what she is doing.

                    JOHN
          Smells good.

                    KATYA
          Thank you. It is an old family
          recipe.

                    JOHN
          Not talkin' about the food.

John kisses her neck.

                    KATYA
               (giggling)
          Stop it. Get yourself a drink. It
          will be ready soon.

John goes to the refrigerator and gets a water
bottle. He hears Katya's cellphone beep. He
walks a little closer as she pulls it out to read
a text message. He sees his name and FBI on the
screen. John freezes for a moment. He then takes
out his own cellphone.

                    JOHN
          Oh damn. I'm getting a call
          from my boss. I'll just take
          it out in the hallway.

                    KATYA
          What? Oh that is OK. You
          don't have to- -

                    JOHN
          I'll be right back.

John quickly puts on his jacket and heads out the
door.

EXT. KATYA'S APARTMENT - DAY
John walks quickly out of the apartment building.
He walks to the street corner and waits for the
light to change. He notices LEV and GRIGORI, tough
looking men in their 20s, across the street looking
at him. He looks to the other side of the street
and sees EMIL looking at him. Emil is a tough but
intelligent looking man in his early 30s with a
scar across his face. Emil points to John and Lev
and Grigori start walking toward him. John turns
and runs in the opposite direction. Emil, Lev, and
Grigori start running after him.

EXT. CITY HALL PARK - DAY

John runs through the park, heading toward the
exit, with his three pursuers close behind. Using
both hands, he vaults over two benches, one after
the other. Emil vaults over the benches with one
hand and Lev hurdles them. Grigori leaps over the
first one, lands awkwardly, stumbles into the
second one, and trips over it, falling down.

John runs across the street just before the light
changes and turns left onto Ann Street. Emil
crosses the street, managing to evade the oncoming
traffic, and follows John. Lev runs into the
street and is struck by a car. He is knocked to the
ground, grabbing his legs in pain.

EXT. ANN STREET - DAY

John runs down the street with Emil following close
behind him. He throws down a garbage can to slow
Emil down, but Emil leaps over it. John runs into
a deserted tunnel. He finds cover in a small
alcove, catches his breath, and pulls a gun from
his jacket. When Emil reaches the corner of the
alcove, John turns out from it and points the gun
at him.

Before he can get off a shot, Emil knocks the gun
out of his hand, punches him in the face, and hits
him again in the ribs. John comes back with a punch
to Emil's face. Emil pulls out a switch blade and

attempts to stab John. John pulls Emil's wrist out
of the way and twists it forcing him to drop the
knife. With his other arm, Emil back fists John in
the face. He then gives John an uppercut to the gut
that drops him to his knees.

Emil pulls out a garrote cable and moves to John's
back. He wraps the cable around John's neck,
strangling him. John struggles against the attack.
Emil lies back on the ground, pulling John with
him, and locking John's legs with his own. John,
pulling against the rope, reaches to his right for
his fallen gun.

When he realizes it is out of reach, he looks to
his left and sees Emil's knife. He reaches for it
and is just able to touch it. He elbows Emil in the
gut which temporarily loosens Emil's grip. John
takes advantage of the distraction. He grabs the
knife and stabs Emil in the chest with it.

John pulls the cable off his neck and rushes to his
feet, gasping for breath and clutching his own
throat. He picks up his gun with his free hand and
points it at Emil. Emil's body falls limp as he dies
from the knife wound.

John drops his arm, still trying to catch his
breath.

Looking to both ends of the tunnel he shoves his
gun back in his jacket and runs out of the end of
the tunnel.

EXT. WALL STREET - NIGHT

The street is deserted except for Control. John
walks up to him.

                    CONTROL
          What the hell happened?

                    JOHN
               (incredulous)
You're asking me? Somebody sold
me out! I'm lucky I got outta
there alive!

                    CONTROL
Back up. Sold you out?
Is it our mole?

                    JOHN
               (trying to calm down)
That's my guess. I was with
Katya. She got a text from
someone. I couldn't make out
the whole thing but I saw my
name and FBI. Next thing I
know I'm running for my life
from these goons.

                    CONTROL
Recognize any of them?

                    JOHN
No. One had a scar across his
face. I... I had to kill him.

                    CONTROL
               (sighs)
So you're blown.

                    JOHN
               (sarcastically)
Pretty sure, yeah.

                    CONTROL
Alright.
               (thinks for a moment)
Alright so we'll dump her phone
which should lead us to our mole.
And we'll try to find some
intelligence on "Scarface". In
the meantime, you lie low.

                    JOHN
          What about Katya?

                    CONTROL
          Stay the hell away from her.
          They've made you. She is no longer
          an asset.

John turns and walks away from Control.

                    JOHN
               (muttering)
          Yeah.

EXT. JOHN'S APARTMENT - NIGHT

John walks up to the apartment and enters the
building.

INT. JOHN'S APARTMENT HALLWAY - NIGHT

John walks up to his door and notices that it has
been broken into. John pulls out his gun, carefully
pushes the door open, and enters the apartment.

INT. JOHN'S APARTMENT - NIGHT

John cautiously enters the apartment, gun at the
ready. He enters the bedroom and finds Katya
holding Renee at gunpoint. Both women have tears
streaming down their faces. John points his gun at
Katya.

                    JOHN
          Katya--What the hell?

                    KATYA
               (hysterical)
          You! You bastard! You killed him!

                    JOHN
          Who...?
                (realizes who)
          Your comrade.

                    KATYA
          My husband!

John is stunned and confused. He lowers his gun
slightly before righting it again.

                    JOHN
          What...

                    KATYA
          Our group suspected you
          were an agent when you
          approached me! They made
          me...

                    JOHN
          You already had a mole why
          did you need--

                    KATYA
          He was in another faction! We
          didn't get his info until later!
          But then my husband...
                (closing her eyes and
                 whispering)
          You bastard.

John notices Renee sobbing.

                    JOHN
          Katya, let her go. You
          don't want her.

                    KATYA
          No! I want you to feel what I
          feel! I want you to lose
          everything!

                    JOHN
          No, Katya--

Katya cocks her pistol and pushes it toward Renee's
head.

                         JOHN
               No!

John fires his gun. The bullet goes through Katya's
head, killing her. Renee screams for a moment. John
lowers his gun, horrified. Renee runs to John and
embraces him. John ignores Renee, looking past her
to Katya with tears in his eyes. Renee notices this
and buries her face in his chest

INT. FBI HEADQUARTERS - DAY

Control is cross referencing Katya's phone records
with the Counter Espionage division. He finds a
match, selects it, and a picture of the mole comes
onscreen.

INT. JOHN'S APARTMENT - DAY

Lev and Grigori burst into the apartment, guns
drawn.

EXT. SOUTH SHORE SEAPORT - DAY

John and Renee walk on the dock toward a boat.

INT. FBI HEADQUARTERS - DAY

Control walks through an office with two agents
behind him. He orders the agents to pull the MOLE
out of his desk chair and place him in handcuffs.

EXT. SOUTH SHORE SEAPORT - DAY

John and Renee stand in front of a boat. Renee
kisses John, but John does not kiss her back. Renee
looks at him, disappointed, then walks toward the
boat.

INT. JOHN'S APARTMENT - DAY

Lev and Grigori move to the bedroom. It is empty
besides Katya's body. When they see the body they
become distraught.

EXT. SOUTH SHORE SEAPORT - DAY

Renee watches John as her boat pulls away from the
dock. John watches the boat leave for a moment. He
then turns around and walks away. He doesn't look
back.

                                        CUT TO BLACK

About the Author

Tyler Kenny is a director, screenwriter and filmmaker. His education includes a Certificate in Film from New York University, a Bachelor's Degree in Film from Hunter College at CUNY and an Associate's Degree in Cinema Studies at Suffolk Community College.

9 789898 599870